This **Chicken House** book belongs to:

....

....

....

To Colin and Edward
may all your best wishes come true!-MM
For Twinnie - CJC

© 2007 The Chicken House

First published in the United Kingdom in 2007 by
The Chicken House, 2 Palmer Street, Frome, Somerset, BA11 1DS
www.doublecluck.com

Text © 2007 Michaela Morgan
Illustrations © 2007 Caroline Jayne Church

Designed by Ian Butterworth

Printed and bound in China by Imago

British Library Cataloguing in Publication Data available
Library of Congress Cataloguing in Publication data available

HB ISBN: 978-1-905294-44-2
PB ISBN: 978-1-905294-72-5

Bunny Wishes

Michaela Morgan

Illustrated by
Caroline Jayne Church

Chicken House

Valenteeny and Valentino (or Teeny and Tino for short) were the closest of friends.

They lived together and shared happy times hopping in the sun and chatting with their friends Mr and Mrs Mouse . . .

. . . and all the new baby mice.

All through the fresh spring days
and the sunny summer days they

hopped and skipped
and frisked and frolicked.

And then the
cold days came . . .

It was winter.

It was a time of squalls and storms, sudden winds and icy chills and finally

SNOW!

Snowflakes,
soft as bunny tails,

fell and tickled noses.
Snow drifted . . .

. . . snow settled.

The world became

crisp and white.

Yippee! Snow!

Everybody loved the snow,
but the new baby mice loved it most of all.
It was their very first snow.

In the dark and icy nights of winter, the two bunnies kept each other warm.

Snug in their burrow they stayed, telling each other stories, singing each other songs, snoozing and dreaming and wishing.

'You know . . .' said Teeny, 'this is a Very Special Time of Year. Your dearest wishes can come true. All you have to do is make a list of everything you want and pin it on to the hollow log.'

'Let's do it! '
they said.

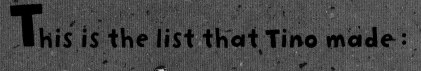

This is the list that Tino made:

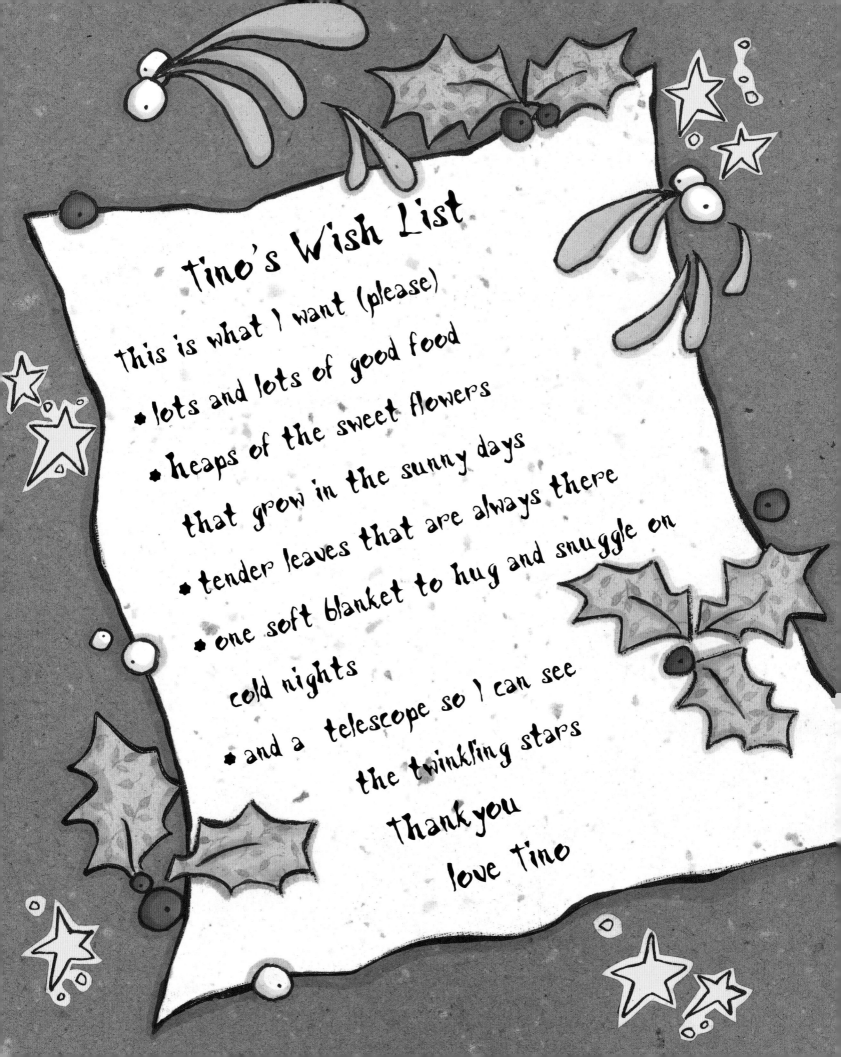

Tino's Wish List

this is what I want (please)

* lots and lots of good food
* heaps of the sweet flowers that grow in the sunny days
* tender leaves that are always there
* one soft blanket to hug and snuggle on cold nights
* and a telescope so I can see the twinkling stars

Thank you
love Tino

And this is the list that Teeny made:

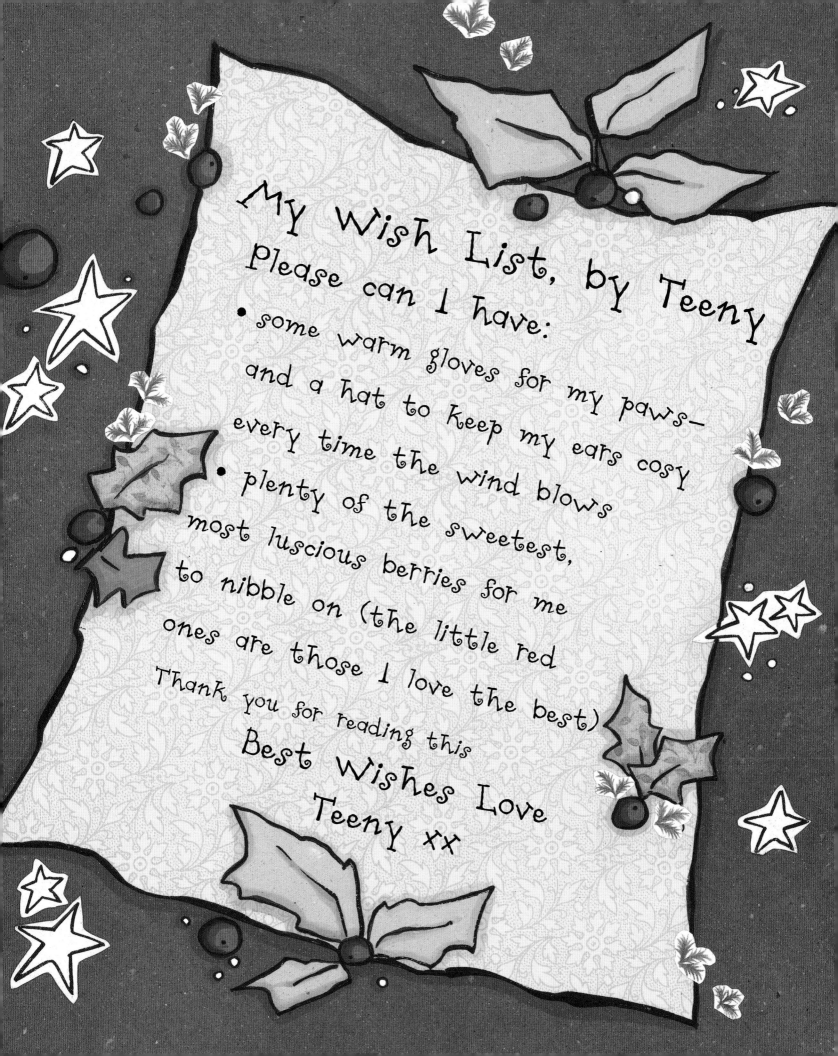

My Wish List, by Teeny

Please can I have:

• some warm gloves for my paws— and a hat to keep my ears cosy every time the wind blows

• plenty of the sweetest, most luscious berries for me to nibble on (the little red ones are those I love the best)

Thank you for reading this

Best Wishes Love
Teeny xx

The two hopeful bunnies hopped over the snowy hill and pinned their lists to the hollow log.

For a while they sat with Mr and Mrs Mouse.
They watched the new baby mice playing
in the snowy distance.

The baby mice loved playing in the snow.
They played with everything they found.
They played with twigs,
stones, leaves and
on the slidey ice.

Whee!

My first
snow mouse!

The bunnies watched and smiled,
then off they hopped - back to
their comfy burrow.

Oof!

An icy wind grew.
First it whistled.
Then it whished.

And then it WHOOSHED!

It whooshed those lists right off the hollow log and into the air . . . .

The letters went up, up and away, round round round round and round and round and then they fell...

But after a while they were very pleased
to find two such big new playthings.

Now they could fly kites,

and make sledges,

and telescopes,

and little hats.

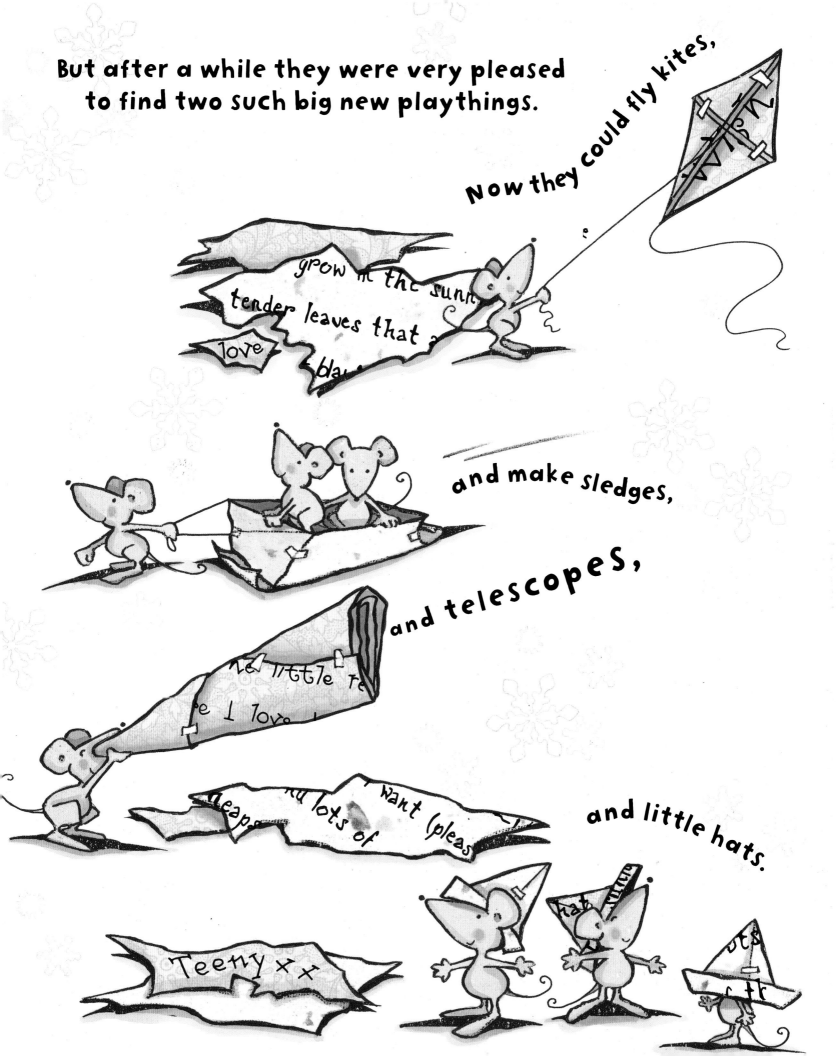

When they were tired of playing,
the little mice toddled
home with their new toys.

I wonder where wishes go?

'Look what we've got!'
said the baby mice

and Mr and Mrs Mouse said,

'OH NOOooooo!'
'You've wrecked the bunnies'
wish lists!'

The bunnies' wishes had been blown away
and toyed with and nibbled at.

The little mice began to cry.

Luckily, Mr and Mrs Mouse knew
EXACTLY what to do to put things right.
They set to work...

Ripping and wrapping and finding and folding licking and sticking planning and wishing and smiling and hugging and kissing.

It was a very BUSY night.

At midnight, when the stars were out,
the mice set off to deliver the wishes.

So when Teeny and Tino
opened their eyes,
this is what they saw.

The bunnies smiled, 'These really are the best wishes we could ever have!' they said.